Y0-DKP-405

THE BASEBALL
BOOK AND TROPHY

By William Humber

Illustrated by Jock MacRae

Somerville House Publishing, Toronto

1

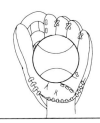

Copyright © 1993
Somerville House Books Limited
All rights reserved. No part of this publication may be reproduced or transmitted
in any form or by any means, electronic, mechanical, including photocopy,
recording or any information storage and retrieval system, without permission in
writing from the publisher.

Canadian Cataloguing-in-Publication Data
Humber, William, 1949-
  The baseball book

GV867.5.H85 1990 j796.357 C89-090760-9
ISBN 0-921051-34-4

Published by Somerville House Publishing
a division of Somerville House Books Limited
3080 Yonge Street, Suite 5000
Toronto, Ontario Canada M4N 3N1

Edited by Susan Hughes

I want to thank the people who helped me in the writing of this book. They
include: my dad, who first taught me the love of baseball as a child, and my
family — my wife Cathie, and our three children, Bradley, Darryl and Karen —
in whom this love continues. Appreciation is due as well to: Hugh Walters of the
Green Diamond Baseball program, Elizabeth Mortlock at Seneca College, and
Susan Hughes, editor of this book. — *Bill Humber*

CONTENTS

A Trophy Right Off the Bat!   **4**

Basic Skills
Day One
Throwing   **6**

Day Two
Catching   **9**

Day Three
Hitting   **14**

Running   **16**

Advanced Play
Take a Break!   **18**

Day Four
The Pitcher   **22**

Day Five
The Batter   **28**

Day Six
The Catcher   **34**

Day Seven
The First Base Position   **40**

Seventh Inning Stretch   **44**

The Second Base Position   **48**

Day Eight
The Shortstop   **52**

The Third Base Position   **55**

Day Nine
The Outfield Position   **60**

Congratulations!   **64**

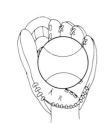

Welcome!

Get set for one of the most wonderful games in the world
— baseball! There are nine exciting innings in a baseball
game, and this baseball program is divided up into nine
days of fun and challenge. You'll need a Coach during
these nine days, so ask someone, maybe a parent, a rela-
tive, or an adult friend, to share your training. Maybe
you'll even go to a baseball game together during your
very own Seventh Inning Stretch!

At the beginning of Day One, right off the bat, your Coach
awards you your trophy. That's to tell you that you're a
star just for trying! Work your way from the basic levels,
Days One to Three, through to the more advanced levels,
Days Four to Nine.

To make the trophy your very own special baseball award,
watch for the sticker symbols at the end of each Day's
program. They tell you that it's time to
collect a sticker and place it on your
trophy. When you've finished all
nine Days and have collected all
nine stickers, your Coach will
sign a special decal with your
name on it that you can place
on the front of your trophy to
remind you that you're a
good sport!

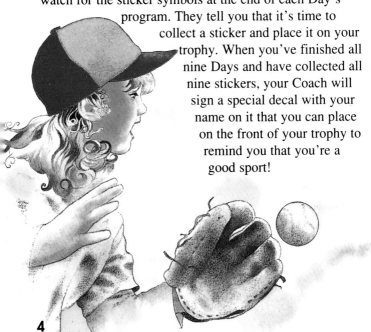

You observe a lot by watching.
—*Yogi Berra*

A Short Cut: The Four Basic Rules

The baseball rule book is more than 100 pages long, but don't worry! You can have fun if you know these few rules:

The batter tries to hit the ball. If he swings and misses three times, he's out. If he hits the ball, he tries to run around the bases and back to home.

If the batter makes it to first base before the ball does, he's safe, and he can keep running or wait until the next play. If a runner touches all the bases and makes it to the fourth base, called home plate, he scores a run.

The players on the other team try to catch fly balls or tag the runners to prevent them from advancing around the bases.

A team is allowed three outs. Then the other team has a chance to score runs at bat.

That's it! Now you're ready to play ball!

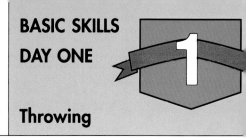
Starting Off Right! The Basics

In the first three Days of this program you'll learn the four basic skills of baseball: throwing, catching, hitting, and running. Try to do the drills with your Coach, and at the end of each Day, don't forget to collect your sticker and put it on your trophy.

Put 'er There: Throwing the Ball

Throwing a ball may look simple, but it takes practice to throw a ball quickly and accurately. Begin by doing the following steps. Then try the two throwing drills.

The Grip

Hold the ball as if it's a bar of soap you're trying to squeeze out of your hand. Rest your fingers across the back of the ball. Use your thumb to grip it on the bottom. Try to keep a small space between the ball and the palm of your hand.

The Throw

 The bow-and-arrow movement:

Grip the ball properly. Now pretend you're going to shoot an arrow from a bow. Bring both your hands in front of you to the same height as your eyes. With your empty or nonthrowing hand, push the bow forward so that this hand

points straight ahead. At the same time, the hand with the ball pulls back the bowstring. Keep your elbow raised above your shoulder. When your throwing hand is just beside your ear, move your shoulders so they are in line with the person you are throwing to. (See illustration A.)

Throwing leg and throwing arm:

Do the bow-and-arrow movement again. This time, as you pull back the string on the bow, step forward with the leg opposite to your throwing arm. Now push your throwing arm forward. (See illustration B.) As the ball passes your head, straighten your arm.

Releasing the ball:

When your hand is past your head and your arm is beginning to straighten, snap your wrist and release the ball. (See illustration C.) Your arm keeps curving until your hand touches your hip. (See illustration D.)

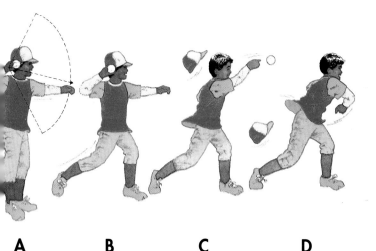

A   B   C   D

All Together Now!
Learning the Proper Throwing Technique

Purpose: To help you concentrate on your grip and the bow-and-arrow movement, without worrying about what your legs should be doing.

What to Do: Get down on your knees, or stand with one foot on a chair rung, and toss the ball back and forth with your Coach. When you feel comfortable throwing the ball like this, stand up with both feet on the ground. Now throw that ball!

A Hole in One: Throwing for Accuracy

Did you know that some professional baseball players can throw a ball almost 100 miles per hour? It's fun to throw a ball hard, but that's not as important as being able to throw a ball so it goes right where you want it to go.

Purpose: To improve your throwing accuracy.

To Prepare: Use chalk to draw several boxes on the wall of a building (with no windows!).

What to Do: Stand close enough to the wall so you can throw the ball and easily hit these boxes. Now back away until you begin to miss the boxes. Mark where you're standing and practice throwing from here until it becomes easy to hit the boxes.

As you improve, move farther and farther back from the wall. With practice, you'll soon be able to throw with speed and with accurate aim. Count the times you get a "hole in one"!

8

2

Catching

I've Got It! I've Got It! Catching the Ball

It's important to learn how to throw, but what do you do when the ball is thrown back to you? You have to catch it! Here's how to practice: Throw a large plastic ball, or even a basketball or volleyball, back and forth with your Coach. Follow these catching tips:

Watch the ball as it flies toward you.

Keep your body in front of the ball.

Eyes on the ball. Use both hands.

Use both hands to catch the ball.

Body in front.

Use your body to keep the ball safe from dropping. After you catch the ball, bring it up against your body.

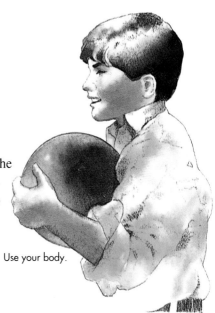

Use your body.

9

Bare Hands: Catching Drills

Purpose: To learn the basics of catching.

What to Do: Play ball toss with your Coach, using a tennis ball. Keep in mind the four catching tips you just learned. Stand close enough together that you can tell baseball stories to each other without needing to raise your voices. Move farther apart as your catching skills improve. You can continue to do this exercise even after you own a glove.

As you get better, try to catch the tennis ball with one hand, the hand you don't throw with. This will be your "glove hand" one day. After you have caught the ball in your glove hand, use the other hand, your throwing hand, too, to hold the ball firmly. This is very similar to what you will do when you begin catching with a glove.

Not Too Big, Not Too Small: Selecting a Glove

Do your hands ever sting when you catch a ball? Now that you've learned the proper ways to catch a ball, it's time to put on a glove and protect your hands. Buy a new glove or scoop one up at a garage sale or goodwill store. Your first glove should be neither too big nor too small. It should fit your hand comfortably.

Take care of your glove and it can last for years! Water isn't good for a glove, and your hand would feel awful if you put it into a rain-soaked glove, so play it safe. Always bring your glove in at night.

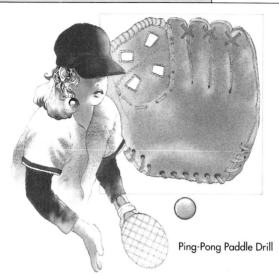

Ping-Pong Paddle Drill

Giving Yourself a Hand:
Two-handed Catching

Imagine that every time you catch a ball, you're clapping for yourself! It'll help you remember to use both hands whenever possible to make a catch. This is your two-handed catch! It lets you throw that ball almost as soon as you catch it, because you don't have to move the ball from your catching hand to your throwing hand!

Purpose: To improve your two-handed catching skills.

To Prepare: Strap a Ping-Pong paddle or a paperback book to your glove hand with electric tape.

What to Do: Catch a tennis ball between the paddle or a paper-back book and your free hand. This will force you to use two hands and will encourage you to get in front of the ball.

A Little History

The earliest forms of baseball go back thousands of years. People living in cold northern Europe waited impatiently all winter for the warm weather to return. When spring came, they played a game with a bat and ball to celebrate. An offshoot of this game was taken to North Africa perhaps 10,000 years ago. It was called *ta kurt om el mahag* or *ball of the mother of the pilgrim,* and it is still played there by desert dwellers.

In Great Britain, in the 1700s, *rounders* was popular. This was a game with five bases. If a player was hit by the ball by a member of the opposing team when he was off base, he was out and had to leave the field. As early as 1820, baseball was played in North America. Each neighborhood or town had its own set of baseball rules. Baseball was thought of as a game for children.

When adults played for fun, they were not very good. They threw in a way that would look funny to you today, and they couldn't throw the ball very far.

Many people believe that baseball with the rules that we know today was

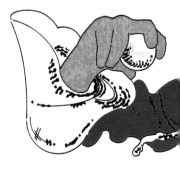

Tomb paintings like these show that the ancient Egyptians played ball games thousands of years ago.

"invented" by an American, Abner Doubleday. It was, in fact, actually developed by a New York bookseller, Alexander Cartwright, in the mid-1840s. He wrote out the first rules that called for nine players on the field a distance of 90 feet between bases, and three outs each inning.

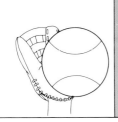

Doing It Right: Hitting the Ball

Hitting a little round ball with a long, narrow piece of wood or aluminum takes skill and practice. If you want to learn how to hit a ball properly, don't always imitate the major league hitters. Major league ballplayers have learned to adjust their bodies and swing to get those hits. You need to learn these basic steps of good hitting before you can adapt your swing to your own strengths.

Selecting the Bat

Hold the bat handle in one hand in a horizontal position in front of you. Keep your arm straight. If your arm shakes, the bat is too heavy. Try this with different bats until you find one that you can hold comfortably.

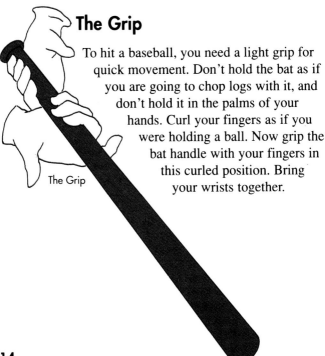

The Grip

To hit a baseball, you need a light grip for quick movement. Don't hold the bat as if you are going to chop logs with it, and don't hold it in the palms of your hands. Curl your fingers as if you were holding a ball. Now grip the bat handle with your fingers in this curled position. Bring your wrists together.

The Grip

The Bat
Only wooden bats are allowed in the major leagues. They are no more than 42 inches long and no more than two and three-quarter inches at the thickest part.

The Hit

With your legs apart, stand sideways to the pitcher. Grip the bat correctly and bend your elbows. The bat should be pointing straight up. Bring it in line with your back shoulder and out from your body. Get ready for the ball. Keep your eyes on the ball, and your head up. (See illustration A.)

When the ball is thrown, shift your weight onto your back foot, as if you were going to hop on it, and move your front leg back a bit. Tilt the top of the bat a little toward the pitcher. (See illustration B.)

Step forward with your front leg and shift your weight onto

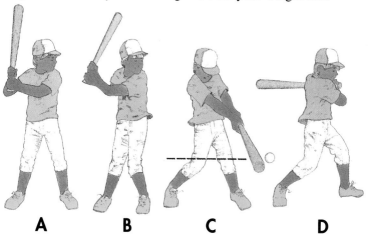

A **B** **C** **D**

it, turning your hips to face the pitcher. Swing the bat to meet the ball so that the top or "head" of the bat moves in a swing that is level to the ground. (See illustration C.)

After you hit the ball, continue to swing. This is called the follow-through. (See illustration D.)

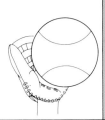

Thinking on Your Toes: Running

The fourth and last basic skill you need is the one you probably already know the most about — running. But do you know when to run and when not to run during a game? Can you tell how fast the ball is moving from one player to another? Do you panic when you are being chased? In baseball, even the fastest runner must learn the basics of running. Here are two games that will make you learn to think on your toes! Ask some friends to play them with you.

Bases: A Running Game

Purpose: To improve your running skills.

To Prepare: You'll need a baseball and at least three players. Mark off two locations, your "bases," that are a comfortable throwing distance apart.

What to Do: One player stands on each base. The third player runs from one base to the other, while the two base players toss the ball back and forth, trying to tag the runner with the ball. The runner scores a point for each base he touches. When he's tagged three times, he switches places with the base player who touched him with the ball the third time.

Prisoner's Base: Another Running Game

Purpose: To improve your running skills.

To Prepare: You'll need two teams of four or more players. Each team has its own base, which is the only place where the team players are "safe."

What to Do: A player from Team 1 leaves the safe base and approaches Team 2's base. A player from Team 2 tries to catch the Team 1 player before that player can run to the safety of his own base. As the Team 2 player comes near Team 1, Team 1 sends out a second player to run after Team 2's player. A new player will continue to run after a new player from the opposite team as each player comes near their safe base. If a player is caught by one team, he becomes a member of that team and must help them to catch other players. The winning team is the one that catches all the other team's players.

CONGRATULATIONS!

3

PLACE STICKER ON TROPHY

ADVANCED PLAY

Take a Break!

Moving On

Now that you know some basic skills, it's time to think about playing a position in a baseball game. This advanced play section of the book will give you some helpful hints about how to prepare for and play the various positions in the field. You'll also pick up six more stickers along the way. But first, take a break, look at the diamond, learn about T-ball, and shake hands with your Coach and your coaches!

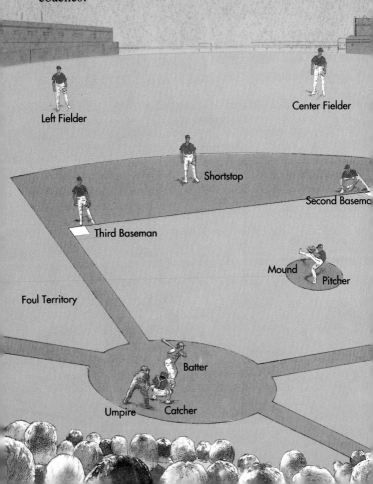

Left Fielder

Center Fielder

Shortstop

Second Baseman

Third Baseman

Mound

Pitcher

Foul Territory

Batter

Umpire   Catcher

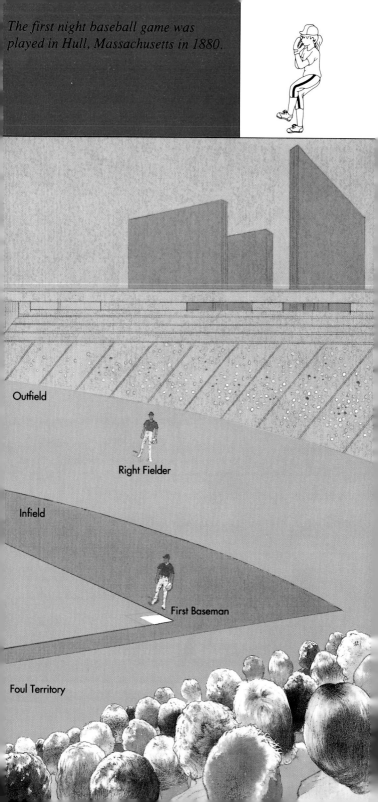

The first night baseball game was played in Hull, Massachusetts in 1880.

Outfield

Right Fielder

Infield

First Baseman

Foul Territory

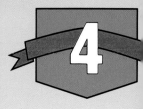

DAY FOUR

The Pitcher

A Good Soup Bone: The Pitcher

Can you throw good pitches and catch, or "field," a lot of balls? Do you have a good "soup bone"? That's a pitcher's throwing arm. In the same way that you can't begin to make a good pot of soup without a good, big bone to add flavor, so you can't begin to have a good team without a pitcher with a good arm! Pitching is a difficult position to play and it can hurt your body, so don't begin to pitch until you're eight or nine years old.

There are two basic pitching motions — the stretch and the full windup. Concentrate on learning the stretch. Once you know it, it's not difficult to add the steps that turn a basic stretch into a windup.

The Grip

To throw a fastball, grip the ball with two fingers across the seam and with your thumb on the bottom. Don't hold the ball in the palm of your hand.

The Grip

The Stretch

Your lead foot is the one opposite to your throwing arm. If you throw with your right arm, your lead foot is your left

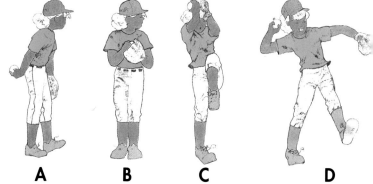

A   **B**   **C**   **D**

Dwight Gooden struck out 276 batters for the New York Mets in 1984 — at the age of 19!

foot. Point it toward the plate and tilt up slightly on your heel. Rest your glove on your knee. With your other hand, hold the ball behind your back. (See illustration A.)

Slide your lead foot back so it is a small footstep from your back foot. Point it toward third base if you are right-handed, and toward first base if you are left-handed. Bring your hands together in front of you at chest level. (See illustration B.)

Swing your lead foot up, lifting your knee as close to your chest as possible. (See illustration C.) Then begin the bow-and-arrow motion, pointing your glove toward home plate and swinging your throwing arm toward second base. (See illustration D.)

Turn your hips toward home and step toward home with your leading foot. Bring your throwing arm forward. Keep your elbow above shoulder level and your throwing arm bent with the ball angled slightly toward your head. Use your legs to drive your body forward. (See illustration E.)

Snap the ball off the ends of your fingers. Your throwing arm follows through past your hip in a downward motion. (See illustrations F and G.)

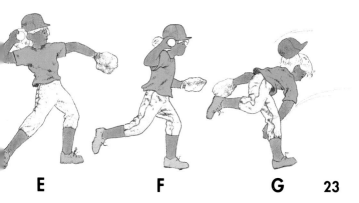

E   **F**   **G**   23

A pitcher who tries to get a batter to swing at a bad pitch "nibbles" or "paints" the edge of the strike zone.

Can You See a Difference?
The Change-of-Pace Pitch

The change-of-pace or change-up pitch is thrown with the same motion as the fastball, and looks just like a fastball, but, in fact, it's a slower pitch. Because the two pitches look so identical, the batter has a difficult time judging when to swing. That's why the change-of-pace pitch is such a useful pitch to learn!

Using the pitching motion you have been practicing, throw a fastball to your Coach. Use the same pitching motion but throw the ball with less force. This is the slower change-of-pace pitch. Keep practicing until you can do both so well that your Coach can't guess which one is coming.

Going for a Walk? The Strike Zone

Where do you aim your pitch? The strike zone is over the home plate (which is 17 inches wide at its widest point) and at a height between the batter's knees and shoulders. (See the illustration on page 28.) If you pitch the ball here and the batter doesn't swing, the umpire will call it a strike.

Purpose: To improve your pitching accuracy.

To Prepare: On the side of a windowless wall, mark in chalk the general area of your strike zone from your knees to your shoulders and 17 inches wide. Divide it into quarters and number each one.

What to Do: Imagine you are pitching to a batter standing at the wall. Practice throwing to all parts of this target. Then throw to the numbered areas called out by your Coach.

Great Pitchers

After pitching a 100.9 mile-per-hour fastball, Nolan Ryan was nicknamed the "Ryan Express" and continued to throw fastballs when he was in his forties.

Nolan Ryan

Cy Young

Between 1890 and 1911, pitcher Denton "Cy" Young won 511 games, an all-time major league record. Today, the year's best pitcher in both the American and National leagues is recognized annually with the Cy Young Award.

An unearned run is a run earned because of an error made by a member of the other team. An earned run is made possible by the pitcher. If a runner gets on base with a hit, a walk, or a hit by the pitcher and scores, this is an earned run. Pitcher Bob "Bullet" Gibson's single season earned run average (E.R.A.) in 1968 for the St. Louis Cardinals was 1.12. In every nine innings he pitched in 1968, he allowed just over one earned run to cross the plate.

Bob Gibson

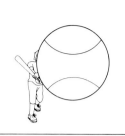

Hit the Wicket: Cricket Baseball

Purpose: To practice your basic pitching skills.

To Prepare: Find two stakes or short sticks of lumber. Get an adult to help you sharpen one end of each stick to a point. Then make a wicket by putting the sticks in the ground so they are at about the height of your waist and about a footstep apart. Balance another stick across them. Make one wicket at home plate and another one about twenty footsteps away.

Cricket Baseball

> *Good pitching will always stop good hitting and vice versa.*
> —Casey Stengel

What to Do: A batter stands in front of the wicket. A pitcher throws to the batter, trying to knock the top stick off the batter's wicket to get the batter out. The batter tries to hit the pitch anywhere into the field and then run around the other wicket and back as many times as possible. The batter gets one point each time he runs around either wicket.

If the pitcher gets the ball and hits the wicket with it while the batter is running between the wickets, the batter is out, and it's the next batter's turn to face the pitcher.

CONGRATULATIONS!
4
PLACE STICKER ON TROPHY

27

Which Way Did It Go? Directing the Ball

An early swing at the ball by a right-handed batter will put the ball into left field. The hit will have a lot of power behind it and may be hard to "field" or catch.

A late swing will send the ball to the opposite field of the swing and probably with less force than a ball hit a little earlier. The ability to hit to all fields is something that even major leaguers try to develop. It is best to master the hit over second base. As you gain experience, you can switch to hitting to the opposite field as a way of confusing the infield.

How Do Major Leaguers Practice?
Some Hints on Hitting

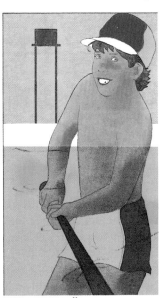

Gregg Jefferies's Tip

To keep your swing smooth, do what infielder Gregg Jefferies does. If you have access to a swimming pool and a lifeguard is on duty, stand chest deep in the water and swing the bat by pulling it through the water as smoothly as possible.

Designated Hitter George Bell practices hitting to different locations. He puts two gloves about six feet apart on the infield, and then tries hitting balls between them like a hockey player shooting on goal.

The Whiffle Ball Toss

Slugger Kevin Mitchell practised by trying to hit a whiffle ball tossed by his grandmother. The ball was hollow, plastic, and sprinkled with holes. It curved and arced in its flight. Hours of hitting the whiffle ball have given Mitchell the confidence to hit a real curveball.

CONGRATULATIONS!

5

PLACE STICKER ON TROPHY

31

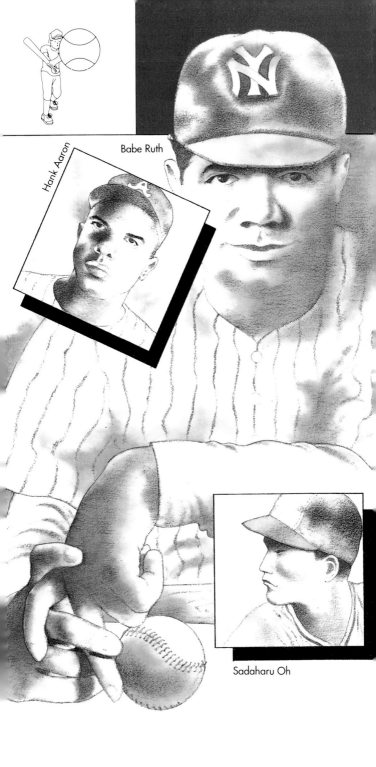

Hank Aaron

Babe Ruth

Sadaharu Oh

Gladys Davis was the leading hitter in the All-American Girls Professional Baseball League in 1943. Baseball's only major league for women lasted until 1954.

Greatest Home Run Hitters

Babe Ruth

Who was early baseball's greatest home run hitter and is now a member of the Baseball Hall of Fame? The Sultan of Swing, the Colossus of Clout, the Bambino, the one and only Babe Ruth! It was Babe Ruth who changed baseball from a pitching game to a game in which fans demanded lots of hits. In 1927, he hit 60 home runs, a record that stood until Roger Maris hit 61 in 1961.

Hank Aaron

In 1947, Jackie Robinson became the first black player allowed in the major leagues in the modern era. Suddenly a stream of other talented young black players could finally aim for the top. One of these players was Hank Aaron. He joined the Milwaukee Braves in 1954. Over the next two decades, he became the greatest North American major league home run hitter, with a total of 755 home runs. To this day, he is the major leagues' leading "runs batted in" (R.B.I.) hitter.

Sadaharu Oh

Can you imagine anyone hitting more home runs than Hank Aaron? No? Well, meet the greatest home run hitter in the world, Sadaharu Oh. He surpassed Hank Aaron's record of 755 home runs in 1977. Oh played his entire career in the Japanese major leagues. His batting style was unusual. Oh's front leg would rise off the ground and bend like a heron's, and often his bat touched his helmet!

33

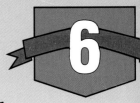
That Masked Man: The Catcher

Who is that masked man? It's the catcher! If you like to squat for stretches of time and can stay quick and alert, this position is for you. Always wear the proper equipment: a mask, a chest protector, shin guards, a bigger, heavily padded glove, and, if you're a boy, an athletic cup. In high-level play, it would be your job to signal to the pitcher which kind of pitch to throw. Because the catcher is the only defensive player who sees the entire field, it can be your job to position your players and remind them of how many strikes and balls the batter has made and how many players are out.

Nerves of Steel: Playing the Position

To be a good catcher, you have to have some of Superman's nerves of steel when that fastball comes flying toward your face. Don't crane your neck to see what is going on. Look out to the pitcher. Keep your bare hand in a soft fist behind your back or leg to protect it from a foul ball until the ball comes into your glove. Always try to squat as close to the plate as is safe. This increases the chance of a thrown or tipped ball landing in your glove or hitting your pads.

It ain't nothin' till I call it.
— Bill Klem, famous umpire

Here, There, Everywhere: A Drill

Purpose: To learn to catch unpredictable pitches.

To Prepare: Get two old chairs with rungs on their backs. Place them on each side of home plate, back to back. Tie a loop of string to the top rung of each chair. Insert a pole or a spare baseball bat through the loops so that it dangles between the chairs and over home plate. Put on your catcher's equipment and take up the catcher's position.

What to Do: Your Coach throws some pitches to you. Sometimes they will come straight to you. Sometimes they may deflect off the pole or bat and require you to scramble for them. Practice catching them or blocking them like a hockey goalie. Tighten or loosen the loops of string to change the height of the pole or bat during some of your drills. The change will keep you guessing and improve your catching skills.

The Final Judge: The Umpire

Who's the second masked man standing behind the catcher? The umpire! He watches the plays in your game and rules on what he sees. He decides whether you are safe or out, or whether the pitch was a ball or strike. In the major leagues, there are four umpires on the field. In your league games, there will likely be two umpires: one behind home plate and one watching the bases.

The umpire also makes sure both teams behave. Always respect the umpire's decisions, especially if you are the catcher. He will not always make the right call, but it is probably better for you or your coach to talk to him after the game if you disagree strongly about a call. No matter what the final decision is, always be a good sport and thank him for helping out.

Up and at 'em! The Running Catcher

If you want to be a catcher, you'd better get out your track shoes and keep doing those running exercises! When the ball is hit and there is no one on base, you have to run down to first base in foul territory and be a backup for the first baseman. Maybe he'll miss a throw from an infielder. If you're nearby, you can try to catch any ball that might get past him. Once the runner has passed first, waste no time getting back to home plate. You may be needed there to protect home plate!

In the big leagues, catchers throw away their masks when the ball is in play. This makes it easier to catch pop flies or catch throws from fielders and tag out runners coming home. In your games, you should leave on your mask. You might need it. Runners are often coming full speed toward home plate, and you need all the protection you can get!

Making the Sure Out:
Inside Baseball Tips

Your games will probably have many runs, because young players usually bat better than they field. Therefore, it is usually best to make what's called "the sure out." What would you do with a runner on third and a ball hit to an infielder? Make the out at first, rather than try to get the runner out at home. With a good lead, even a major league team will often give up the run at home to get the sure out at the bases.

What if it's the bottom of the last inning with the score tied and one out? The infielder may get a runner out on a base, but while this is happening, a runner could score at home plate. Because the score is very important in this situation, the infielder should throw to home and try to stop the runner from scoring, even if the other runner advances closer to home plate.

Why is it important for the catcher to learn these tips? It's the catcher's job to alert his fielders and point out the changing situations during a game.

CONGRATULATIONS!

6

PLACE STICKER ON TROPHY

37

Where Are Major League Baseball Players Born?

Most major league ball-players come from places with warm climates. California is first on the list. Outside of the United States, the Dominican Republic is one of the leading countries from which major leaguers come. There are always about five Canadians in the big leagues each year, proving that cold winters can be overcome!

Perhaps the most unusual birthplace was that of Ed Porray of Buffalo's Federal League team in 1914. Born in 1888, his place of birth is listed as the "Atlantic Ocean"! There is a good reason though. Porray's parents were immigrating to North America on a ship when he was born!

Baseball Cards

Who hasn't bought flat cardboard-tasting gum just to get the baseball cards that are in the package with them? The first baseball cards were produced over 100 years ago and were cheap to buy. Now some of these cards are very valuable. Mickey Mantle's 1952 Topps card has been valued up to $50,000. Honus Wagner's 1910 card may be worth more than a half million dollars because so few of these cards were produced.

Today many companies produce different sizes and types of cards, and baseball-card collecting is still a fun hobby. Why not try it? And here's a tip. Hang on to cards of rookie players. They may be valuable in years to come if the player becomes a great star!

Honus Wagner, 1910

Dave Winfield, 1988

Dennis Rasmussen, 1988

39

Cutting It Close: The First Base

If you want a position with a lot of excitement and action, be a first baseman. You will have to stop ground balls and, more importantly, catch balls thrown from any infield position and tag the bag before the batter reaches it. There are more close plays at first than at any other position. You should concentrate on making the catch and then holding the ball securely. Often a player is so busy thinking about getting back to the bag that the ball will hit his glove and roll away as he turns back to the bag! Try these exercises and read the tips and then, if you're not too exhausted, collect your sticker!

Leave the Bag or Leave the Ball?
Tips for the First Baseman

Sometimes the long toss from third to first can go wide. If this happens, leave the bag to get the ball. You'll probably have time to get back and tag the base before the runner gets there. If you don't make the catch, the ball can go past you into foul territory or out into right field, and the batter might run on to the next base. By making sure you make the catch, you prevent the runner from going on.

Catching a Bouncing Ball:
Fielding Grounders Drill

A grounder is a ball that hits the ground and bounces. Most ground balls are hit to the left side of the infield between second and third bases, but some will find their way to you on first base. Your job is to make sure the ball doesn't go past you.

Purpose: To practice catching grounders.

What to Do: Your Coach bounces ground balls to you. Get down on one knee to catch the balls. When you're on one knee, the ball has less chance of going between your legs if you miss it. Don't worry if you don't catch the ball. You are doing well if you can keep it in front of you.

Ready for Anything: Waiting for the Pitch

As the pitcher takes his warm-up, you must stand alert and poised, like a cat about to spring. Lean forward on your toes, bend your knees as if you were about to do a standing broad jump, and get your glove and throwing hand down. With the palm of the open hand facing the open glove, you will be ready for a ground ball.

If there is no runner on first, stand well off and behind the bag, a little toward second base. If the ball is hit to the left

The Fielding Position

side of the infield, there's plenty of time to get over to first to take the fielder's throw. If the ball is hit to your side of the infield, try for it. The pitcher should cover first to take your throw. If there is a runner on first, stand behind him with one foot on either side of the bag, but don't interfere with the runner. Be prepared for your pitcher to toss the ball to you. If you're quick enough, you and the pitcher might pick the runner off first. If the pitcher throws to home, move off the base and get ready in case a ground ball is hit your way.

It's in the Bag! Making a Bag for a Base

Make a first base bag for your practice drills. Sometimes seat cushions are given away at ball games. If you have two or three of them, wrap them together with electric tape, and you've got a good bag.

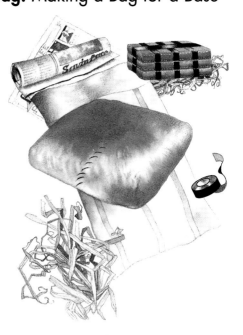

A Homemade First Base Bag

If you don't have any seat cushions, collect straw, shredded paper, or foam from packages, or ask a parent for any extra rags. Fill an old pillowcase with these materials, sew or staple it tight, and your bag is ready to be stomped on!

Where's the Bag? A Drill

Purpose: To learn how to reach out with your foot from wherever you are and step on the first base bag while catching the ball.

To Prepare: Put your new bag behind you.

What to Do: Your Coach tosses the ball, first directly to you, then to your right or left. After you catch each toss, try to touch the bag with the leg opposite to your glove hand. Don't look behind you at the bag. Get comfortable with the idea of first making the catch and then finding the bag. Then practice doing both at the same time. As the ball is thrown, reach back with your leg and out with your glove hand. Soon you will be doing this easily. But remember: Which do you choose to do if you can't touch the bag *and* make the catch? You concentrate on making the catch.

Tips for the Runner Going to First Base:
A Simple Running Drill

Purpose: To learn how to run quickly to first base.

To Prepare: Go to a baseball diamond, or set up a home plate bag and first base bag in your backyard.

What to Do: Your Coach times you as you run as fast as you can from home plate:

to a point about 20 strides beyond first base, keeping your eyes on that point.

directly to the first base bag, keeping your eyes on it.

directly to the first base bag, with your head turned, looking at the shortstop position.

Did you discover that when you run directly to the first base bag and stop right on it, you slow yourself down before you reach the bag? And turning your head away from where you are running has the same result? The fastest way to run to first is the first way.

Take Me Out to the Ball Game:
It's Fun to Watch

In the middle of the seventh inning of a baseball game, after the visiting team has been up to bat but before the home team is up to bat, it's time for the Seventh Inning Stretch. Everyone is invited to stand up and stretch and get ready for more action in the final innings to come! Your Seventh Inning Stretch comes in the middle of your Day Seven program. Stretch *your* legs by going to a baseball game with your Coach!

Enjoy the Game!

Try to get there early so that you can see batting practice. You can learn a lot from the way ballplayers prepare for a game. If you're lucky, some ballplayers might wander over to the side of the field and sign your autograph book.

Bring a scorecard, or buy a program.

The number seven has always been considered lucky, and that's why fans stand and stretch in that inning.

Bring your glove. A ball hit into the stands might bounce near you.

Wear the cap of your favorite team — and protect your head from the summer sun.

Holler out advice to the team you're rooting for!

Watch the pitcher's windup when there are no runners on base. See how it changes when there *are* runners on base.

Count the number of pitches thrown in the inning. Is the first pitch usually a strike or a ball? If the pitcher is throwing more than 15 or 20 pitches per inning, and his first pitch to a batter is often a ball, he may not be in the game very long.

After the Game:
A Scrapbook

Start a baseball scrapbook. In it, put the ticket stub from the game. Clip out the box score of the game in the next day's newspaper and put it in your scrapbook along with some baseball cards of the players you saw in the game.

45

Songs and Candy

While riding the New York subway, Jack Norworth saw an advertisement for a ball game. He had never seen a baseball game in his life, but he liked the ad so much, he wrote the famous song "Take Me Out to the Ball Game."

long, skinny dachshund dog. A cartoonist drawing the sausage and bun was not sure of how to spell dachshund, so instead he wrote the words "hot dog" on his cartoon. It stuck, and that's what it's been called ever since!

"Take Me Out to the Ball Game."

In Norworth's song, fans are eating peanuts and Cracker Jack. Cracker Jack is still popular today, especially at ball games. It was invented by two brothers living in Chicago. They mixed popcorn, peanuts, and molasses in a rotating barrel to keep it from sticking. In 1893, they told a salesman about their new product, and he replied, "That's a cracker jack of an idea." It stuck. And so does Cracker Jack!

Fancy Footwork: The Second Base

Are you a good dancer? Then maybe this position is for you. As a second baseman, you will play on the first base side of second base. Your main job is to catch grounders and throw them to first base. You can go down on one knee to stop the ball either with the glove or your body and then stand and throw out the runner at first.

A Quiz: Second Base Rules

Try this multiple-choice quiz and see how you score.

1 A Force Play

You are the second baseman. The batter hits the ball on the ground to second base. The runner on first base must run as soon as the ball is hit because the batter must run to first. This is called a force play. What do you do if you are the second baseman and you have caught the ball?

a) Run to second with the ball.

b) Toss the ball to a shortstop covering second.

c) Throw the ball to first to catch the hitter out, and let the runner from first reach second.

All the above answers are correct. A runner in a force play does not need to be tagged. If the ball is held by the second baseman on second base before the runner gets there, the runner is out.

2 The Infield Fly Rule

You are the second baseman. Runners are on first and second base, and one player is out. The ball is hit in the air to you. What should you do?

48

a) Let the ball drop. If the runners think the ball will be a fly ball, they will stay on their bases. If you pick up the ball after it bounces and throw it to third, you can get one of them out on a force play.

b) Try to make the catch, because whether you do or not, the batter is out.

The correct answer is (b), because of the Infield Fly rule. The rule is: If a batter hits a fly ball into the infield with runners on the bases, with fewer than two players out, he is out, even if the fly is not caught by an infielder before it bounces. A runner may stay on base or run. However, if he runs, he can be tagged out. Before this rule was made, a runner in this situation was helpless. If he stayed on base and the fielder dropped the ball, he could be retired on a force play. If he left the base and the ball was caught and thrown to the base before he could return to it, he could be retired.

Over or Under?
Special Fielding Tips for Second Basemen

If the ball is hit to your left (the first base side), it can be faster for you to toss the ball underhand to first than to stand up and throw overhand.

Purpose: To practice your underhand toss.

To Prepare: Set up a bucket where first base would be.

What to Do: Your Coach hits balls to your left side. Field the balls, then see how many you can throw with an underhand toss into the bucket.

Next time that someone tells you an "ivory hunter" is in the stands, play your best. These hunters are major league scouts.

Going Up? Catching the Ground Ball

You have practiced fielding plays by going down on one knee. Most ground balls, however, will be fielded with knees bent and not touching the ground. The key to catching a grounder is not to stand still and wait for the ball to arrive in your glove, because it might not happen! A bouncing ball can hit a pebble and bounce over your head.

To catch a ground ball, you need to stand in the ready position before the pitch is made. When a grounder is hit, move in on it, and try to keep your body in front of it. Keep your legs slightly bent. Your knees don't touch the ground. Use both hands to scoop the ball up into your body. Now make the throw to a base.

An easy way to practice catching grounders is to toss a ball against a wall, run in, and field it on the bounce.

Not Only on Ice! Sliding to Second Base

You're running to second. The ball is in the air. The second baseman almost has it. It's going to be close. What do you do? Sliiiiiide . . . ! Sliding into second base is a common play, but you have to know how to do it. It's not like sliding on ice!

As you approach the bag, keep your eyes on the base.

Take off on your strongest leg, probably your right one. Bend it under your other leg so that both legs form the shape of the figure 4.

Sit down as you raise your opposite leg well off the ground. (See illustration A)

Keep your hands up, and slide on your lower hip. Don't forget to touch the bag with your foot! (See illustration B)

Sliiiiiiiiiiiiide! **B**

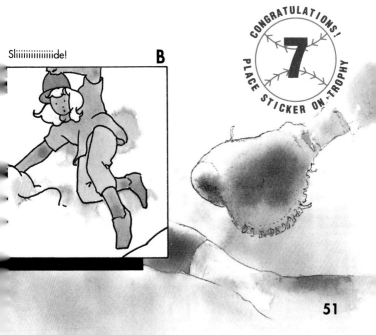

CONGRATULATIONS!
7
PLACE STICKER ON TROPHY

A Little Bit of Everything: The Shortstop

Are you good at a little bit of everything? Maybe you should be a shortstop. You will play more ground balls than anyone else, and many of the fly balls in the game will come your way.

It is your job to run into left field when the ball is hit in that direction. You must be ready to receive the ball from the outfielder and throw it into the infield. When there is a hit to right field and the second baseman goes out to take the throw, you, the shortstop, must even cover second base!

The Crow Hop

Doing the Crow Hop:
Throwing to First Base

Is it a strange new dance? No. It's simply the best way to throw the ball when you've fielded it and want to throw to first. Try it and then practice it a few times. Brace your back foot. While you step forward with your throwing foot, push off on your back foot. Take a little hop onto the front foot as you release the ball.

To Stretch or Not to Stretch:
Difficult Ground Balls

Not all ground balls will be hit directly to you. Always run to the place where the ball is headed. Keep your glove down, and try to get in front of the ball. If you can't, stretch for it, but don't get in the habit of running with your glove outstretched all the time. You'll have trouble seeing the ball, and you can't run as well this way.

Here are three situations where you, the shortstop, may need to stretch for the ball:

If a ball is hit to your glove-hand side, you may need to reach out your glove to make the catch. Then bring the ball into your body, turn your body sideways to first base, plant your feet, and make the throw.

A ball hit to your throwing-hand side is a difficult play. You must run with the glove reaching across your body and make the catch back-handed with the thumb of your glove pointing down. Then stop quickly, anchor your back leg, and make a hard overhand throw to the base.

How do you catch a slow-rolling ground ball? Don't wait — charge it. Bend your knees slightly with both your hands down. Scoop the ball up to your body elevator-style and make the throw to first.

The Third Base Position

Time to Stre-e-e-e-tch: A Drill

Purpose: To learn when to stretch for the ball and when not to.

To Prepare: Find a hard, level surface where the ball won't take too many unpredictable bounces.

What to Do: Begin with stretching exercises. Then your Coach hits ground balls to either side of you and slow rollers in front of you. Your Coach can tell you when you were correct to stretch and when you should have tried harder to get your body in front of the ball.

Follow the Bouncing Ball: Different Landing Surfaces

Where will the ball bounce if it lands . . . ?

On grass. A fly ball hitting grass will have less bounce than if it lands on any other surface. It can roll or hit a rut in the ground and go in strange directions.

In dirt. A fly ball hitting dirt will likely bounce, especially if the field is quite dry. A rolling ball will usually bounce true, but watch out for nicks or stones that can deflect the ball.

On gravel. A fly ball hitting gravel will probably die, but a bouncing ball can go anywhere! Play a grounder as soon as possible, before it can deflect past you.

On concrete. A fly ball hitting concrete may bounce over your head. A grounder will usually bounce true, but it will move faster than if it hits gravel or grass.

When you consider that 75 percent of the play is in the infield, you realize how much tougher it is to play there.
— *Ron "Penguin" Cey, former Los Angeles Dodgers infielder*

The Hot Corner: The Third Baseman

Are you ready to play the "hot corner"? This is not really a place where the sun beats down stronger. The "hot corner" is third base. It gets its name because ground balls hit to third are usually difficult to handle.

As the third baseman, you play closer to the batter than any other infielder, except the pitcher. With players on base, you must be able to touch third if the runner on second is forced to go there. You must be able to throw home if the runner on third is forced to go there. If there are no force plays at home or third, it is usually better for you to throw to first. Throwing to first is a long throw, so you must have a good and generally accurate arm.

Looking Home:
Tips to the Third Base Runner

Always be alert to what is happening around you. Often there are opportunities for you to run to or "steal" home when the ball is being thrown back and forth between the catcher and the pitcher.

On a wild pitch, the ball may bounce far enough away from the catcher to allow you to run home.

If a pitch bounces only a short distance from the catcher, and he throws it back to the pitcher immediately, run for home. It is very difficult for the catcher to get back into position, take the return throw from the pitcher, and tag you out.

If the throw from the catcher back to the pitcher goes over his head and out past second base, try to run home.

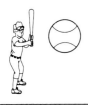

Around 1912, the King of England hired a former big leaguer to be his personal baseball instructor after watching a touring group of Americans play the game!

Talk It Up! The Baseball Code

When you play infield, you are usually quite close to your teammates, and they can easily hear you yell out encouraging things. This infield chatter is a tradition of baseball. Players have been inventing and calling out their own favorite expressions for a long time. Try making up some of your own!

Bring that good hard cheese	Pitch your fastball
Set down the side	Get three outs
Throw your old bread and butter	Use your best pitch
Work all the sides	Pitch to both sides of the plate
Throw BBs	Throw your fastest pitch
Go downtown/Hit a tater	Hit a home run
Spoil his pitch	Foul off a pitch
Free ticket	Our batter is walked
You're in the launching pad	You're ready to hit one
Hit a rope	Hit a line drive
You brought your leather today	You made a good play with the glove
Can of corn	Easy fly ball catch
Go airborne	Jump for a line drive

Around the horn	Do some warm-up tosses from third to second to first and back
Gun it	Throw him out

A Fielding Tip:
Wear a batting glove under your fielding glove to help break the sting of the ball.

Look Way Up:
It's hard to see a ball against a blue or slightly cloudy sky. That's why fielders prefer to play ball when the sky is dull and gray.

> *Good pitching isn't worth anything without good fielding.*
> — *Ken "Hawk" Harrelson, former Boston Red Sox player*

What a Catch!

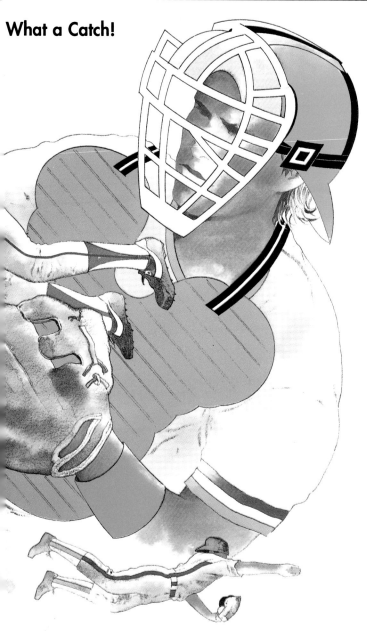

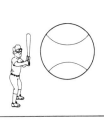

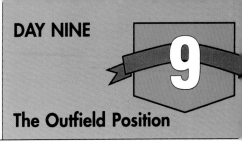
The Last Line of Defense:
The Outfielder

Look at those amazing outfielders' catches on pages 58 and 59. If you can catch fly balls, or stop ground balls that have gone through or over the infield, if you like people to depend on you, and if you like being the one who saves the day when all else fails, then an outfield position sounds right for you! Whether you are in the left, right, or center field position, you are the last line of defense in a baseball game.

Making the Sure Stop:
Catching Bouncing Balls

Always position yourself well before the ball is hit. Keep an eye on your coaches. They may decide to move you in or out, to your right or left, depending on which player is hitting.

The batter hits a slow ground ball through the infield. Before you think about catching the ball, think about stopping it. It's your job to prevent the ball getting past you for an almost sure home run. Get your body in front of the ball. Then go down on one knee for the catch, as if you were fielding at first or second. It may take longer to get the ball back to the infield, because you'll have to stand up again to make the throw, but this is the way to make a sure stop. Go back to the sections on fielding ground balls (pages 40-41) for some good practice ideas.

When you feel more confident, you may want to catch the ball with your knees only slightly bent, so that you can return the ball back into the infield as quickly as possible.

I owe my success to a fast outfield.
— *Lefty Gomez, former New York Yankees pitcher*

Which Way Did It Go?
Catching Fly Balls

It looks easy, but learning to catch fly balls takes a lot of practice. At first, you must always keep your eye on the ball. But often you'll have to run to where you think the ball is going. Can you run and watch the ball at the same time? Sure, but there's a better way to catch a fly ball.

Purpose: To practice catching fly balls. (Don't try this until you have very good catching skills.)

What to Do: Your Coach tosses a ball up in the air. Watch it for a few seconds, look away for a few seconds, then look back again and try to refocus on the ball. When you can do this, your Coach throws the ball high and close to you. With your eyes off the ball, take a few steps in the direction of the ball, and then try to refocus on it.

Purpose: To prepare catching flies in game play.

What to Do: When your Coach throws the ball, judge where it is going. Run to the location, keeping your eyes either on that location or on the ball, depending on your skill level. Don't stretch out your arms.

Yell out that you are going to catch the ball. Whoever calls first, makes the catch. This prevents collisions with other outfielders.

Prepare to catch the ball. Raise both your arms so that when the ball falls into your glove, you can quickly switch it to your throwing hand.

The Most Famous Catch in History

It's the eighth inning of the first game of the 1954 World Series. Willie Mays of the New York Giants runs after Vic Wertz's long drive. A whole 425 feet from home plate, Mays catches the ball!

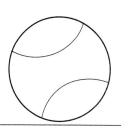

Keep Moving:
Backing Up Your Teammates

Many times during a game there is not much action in the outfield. There may be very few hits that reach your position. But you can help your team by running when the ball is put in play. For instance, a ground ball in the infield on your side of the outfield may get past the infielder. You can help by running in to be his backup.

If the ball is hit in the air or on the ground to the left or right fielder, the center fielder should run to a position behind that fielder. He may be able to make a play if his teammate misses the ball.

If the ball is hit to right field, the left fielder moves to back up either second or third base, in case the right outfielder's relay throw to the infield gets past the shortstop or third baseman.

If stealing or leadoffs are allowed in your games, the pitcher may throw to the first or second baseman, hoping to catch the runner off base. If the baseman misses the ball, the outfielder must get the ball back to the infield before the runner can score.

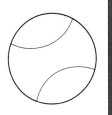

PLAY BALL!

Congratulations! You have successfully completed the Nine-Day Basic Ball Program. Now it's time for your Coach to put your name on the decal for the front of your trophy. Your Coach will sign it, too! Take a moment with your Coach to look at the stickers you've earned. Each one of them shows you've tried your best to improve your catching, throwing, batting, and running skills. But remember, there's lots of baseball fun ahead of you, and you can go back through the pages of this book anytime and practice the drills over and over again to further improve your skills.

Enjoy your trophy and show it to your friends. Your baseball future is off to a great start! Play ball!

Author William Humber, baseball historian, player, coach, and father of three baseball enthusiasts, lives near Toronto, Ontario – home of the 1992 World Series champion Blue Jays.